WHALE IN THE SKY

WHALE IN THE SKY
by Anne Siberell

A PUFFIN UNICORN

to GEPS

Copyright © 1982 by Anne Siberell
All rights reserved.
Unicorn is a registered trademark of Dutton Children's Books
Library of Congress number 82-2483
ISBN 0-14-054792-4
Published in the United States by Dutton Children's Books,
a division of Penguin Books USA Inc.
Editor: Emilie McLeod   Designer: Claire Counihan
Printed in Hong Kong by South China Printing Co.
W
10

Long ago, the rivers and sea were filled with fish,
and tall trees crowded the mountainsides. There
was no written language among the Indian tribes
of the Northwest, and storytellers passed history
and legends from one generation to the next.
Sometimes a chief would hire an artist to carve
a story in pictures on the trunk of a giant tree.
Whale in the Sky is such a tale.

The carved tree, called a totem pole, identified
the chief and his family, his clan and tribe.

In a time long ago, Thunderbird watched over
the sea and land and all its creatures.

One day he saw Whale, small on the horizon
of the sea. He did not see Frog, small on the
bank of the river.

Frog trembled because Whale was growing larger.
The salmon swam faster and faster as Whale chased
them through the sea and into the river.

Whale chased the salmon up the river,
and Frog was afraid.

He called to Raven.

Raven flew into the sky after Thunderbird.

"Whale swallows the salmon and chases them into the river," he called.

Thunderbird stretched his great wings wide
and flew like the wind.

He saw Whale in the river.

He grabbed Whale in his terrible talons and flew
high into the sky. Whale struggled and screamed.

Thunderbird flew higher and higher. Then he
dropped Whale on the highest mountain.

Frog was safe. He thanked his friend Raven.
Now there were salmon for the people
who lived beside the river.

Whale gasped and shivered on the mountain.
He promised to stay out of the river
if he could return to the sea.

Thunderbird clapped his great wings, and
Whale slid down the mountain, back to the sea.

The chief of the people told this tale
to the carver. The carver made the story
into a totem pole.

Thunderbird holds Whale, while Raven
watches over Salmon and Frog.

THE CARVER'S TOOLS

Adzes of jadeite, a hard stone, with wood handles

Wedges

Mallet-like *hammers* of wood

Chisels of stone or bone

Rough, dried *sharkskin* for smoothing

Glue from boiled halibut fins

Modern totem poles are carved with steel-bladed knives.

COLORS

Black and *gray* were made from charcoal, manganese or graphite, mixed with fish oil, animal oil or chewed salmon eggs.

Brown, from bear dung or chewed cedar bark with oils

Green, copper scraped from rocks and soaked in urine

Yellow, from decayed moss and fungus with oils

Red, from berries and animal blood, mixed with oils

Purple, from berries

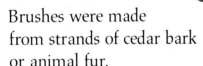

Brushes were made from strands of cedar bark or animal fur.

The colors were mixed in stone dishes.

White, from crushed clamshells